P9-CMO-580

the Lost Boy

GREG RUTH

graphix

An Imprint of

SCHOLASTIC

For David Saylor, who kept this book afloat
through foul, fair, and furious weather. And for Adam
Rau, who brought it in to harbor at last.

All rights reserved. Published by Graphix, an imprint of Scholastic Inc.,
Publishers since 1920. SCHOLASTIC, GRAPHIX, and associated logos are
trademarks and/or registered trademarks of Scholastic Inc.

Library of Congress Control Number: 2013937147

ISBN 978-0-439-82331-9 (hardcover)
ISBN 978-0-439-82332-6 (paperback)
12 11 10 9 8 7 6 5 4 3 2 1   13 14 15 16 17
Printed in China   38

First edition, September 2013
Edited by Adam Rau
Book design by Phil Falco
Creative Director: David Saylor

Part One
Walt

3

4

Man, oh man...

7

9

CLAK!
KLACK!
CLAK!
CLAK!

Darn it!

No!

...No.

You've found it, I see.

Huh?

The room. You picked a *good* one.

Oh... yeah. I *guess*.

Wow--now, *that's* a relic from the *past*.

...

It just sorta... *stopped*.

Hmm...

Probably just a bad *spring*.

I bet we can *steal* one off that old switch plate across the hall.

Come on.

16

Perfect! See how that *switch* controls the tension?

Yeah... and that knob starts up the *motor*, right?

Exactly.

Looks like the *contacts* will need a cleaning, too...

...but save that for *another* time. You're *good* to go for now.

Thanks, Dad.

You *bet*, Champ.

Just take it *easy* until we can get a proper spring in--

PROPERTY OF: WALTER PIDGIN TOP SECRET!

Oh... hello!

Hey!

PROPERTY OF:
WALTER PIDGIN
TOP SECRET!

click

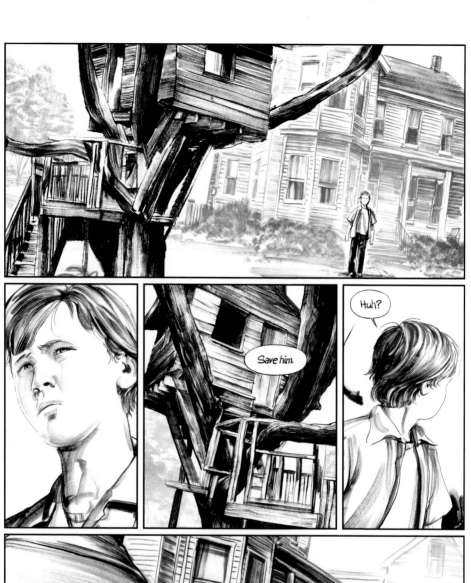

No way.

I don't...
What are
you--

Wait!

Come
back!

Hang on!
I just want--

Oh...kay.

37

This doesn't have *any* rings at all.

None of them do.

Okay, so that means they're *young*, right?

Yeah... young as in grown *today*.

But... some of these branches are as thick as my *leg*.

How could they have *possibly* been grown *today*?

Someone left a *huge* pile of twigs near our back door yesterday...

...Mom just assumed it was the neighbors.

Given where *you* live, you're probably *right*.

Wait! What does *that* mean?

Hey!

55

Poor Walt.

What? He tore into that dude like an *animal!*

Who does something like that?

FLIP

FLIP

Someone who's trying to *protect* himself from a *bully*.

...*Oh* so this is some kind of *macho guy* thing, then.

You've done this *yourself*, I suppose.

No! Of *course* not.

Not everything's so *black-and-white*, Tabitha.

And you say you found this here under the floorboards?

Yeah, *so*?

So?

Nate... the police report says the *cops* found the *recorder* in Walt's *tree house*.

And how did *you* get your hands on a *police report* anyway?

Never mind *that*. Doesn't this *worry* you?

That your life of *crime* will eventually end with you in jail? Yes.

No, dufus...

...it means *we're* just playing someone else's *game*.

58

62

...Lucky for *me*, my room's on the *first* floor.

I *knew* it wasn't a *dream*...

So *you* saw it *too*...

Yeah...

But *how* could it be in two *different* places at *once*?

Who knows?

I wasn't sticking around to ask it *questions*.

Oh my *GOD*... My mom must think I'm *dead* or something.

I have to get *back!*

Wait! Hang on.

65

Aya, Tamalane... aya, Plikt.

What did you find out?

So *that's* what all the *noise* was about.

Hmmm...

You're *certain?* And still no sign of *Tom?*

Warr... tik corr!

Okay... Calm *down*-- no need to get your *roots* in a *twist.*

But I will *not* make the same mistake *twice.* We will wait for *Tom* this time.

68

click

Part Two
Nate & Tabitha

So... Walt wasn't *kidnapped* after all.

Nate...

...we just solved a riddle that's been driving this town *crazy* for half a century.

And it's not even *lunch-time* yet.

So...

What *now?* We take this to the police?

NO way. At least not *yet.* There might be something *else* in here that we can use against whatever's going on *now.*

Okay. That makes sense.

Do you think... he could *still* be out there?

Walt? No way. We'd have *heard* something by now. He's *gone,* Nate.

I guess you're *right*...

...but there's a *connection* between what happened to Walt and what's going on. now. I can *feel* it.

First thing we should do is figure out *who* left the recorder in my room--

Well, I can answer *that* at least.

The Shadows' agent in our world.

The *Vespertine*.

So that was the...*thing* that attacked us last night.

Yes... *no!*

Not *exactly*. What you saw were ...*puppets*. Copies of himself.

It is.... one of his *talents*.

He can... *project* his will through *any* nearby foliage...but it is *very* taxing.

He will... *continue* this madness until the *Gate Key* is found.

But why does he think *we* have it?

He believes I have *given* it to you.

But you *didn't*.

True....but he is *insane* with rage.

He desires only to unleash a war of *vengeance* on your town.

There's... some really *weird* stuff in here, Tabitha.

This just... *wiggled.*

I'd put it *down.*

Who knows *what's* hidden away in--

Mind the *oolong!*

H-Haloran! You're not... *dead.*

Such a *charmer!*

But you are *correct.* I am presently *alive.*

Alas... the same *cannot* be said of my *tea.*

Sorry... I didn't see you there.

Never you *mind,* dear. It was *my* fault for *sneaking* up on you.

But... shouldn't you be... *older?* Like ancient?

Longevity is just one of the burdens of my... *office.*

But let's not do this *here.* Everyone's waiting *upstairs.*

Tabitha?

Plikt...

Where's Tamalane?

Gone.

They'll take her back to the *Vespertine.*

And... *then* what?

They'll *execute* her.

Publicly. As a *lesson* to others.

Haloran, we have to *stop* it.

She would not show *you* the same kindness, Nate.

That's why we have to do it.

We have to *end* this before anyone else gets *hurt*.

I *know*...but there's nothing we can *do*. They're halfway to the *Barrowlands* by now.

No. I don't just mean Tamalane. It's *long* past time we put a stop to *all* of this.

Nate's *right*. We have to start getting out in *front* of this situation before *we're* next.

We need a *plan*.

Look, the Vespertine thinks we have the Key, *right?*

We can't prove we *don't*, so let's stop trying to and use it to our *advantage*.

I'm almost afraid to ask *how*...

We go *into* Crow's Woods. We bring the *fight* to him.

Nate.

I *admire* your spirit, but you two wouldn't last half a *day* in The Kingdom alone.

Then *you'll* have to come *with* us, Haloran.

Tom, too.

Nate... slow down. We need to think this through.

They're *late*.

They're *late* because they've been *eaten*, and we're *sitting ducks* out here, waiting to be *next*.

Relax, Nate. You're *spinning*.

It's a good plan. A crazy, suicide, *lunatic* plan, but still, a good one.

Uh-oh.

"Uh-oh"? *What* "uh-oh"?

There... Over by the garbage cans.

Oh *God*, Tabitha. We are *toast*.

And is it *me*, or are there a lot more *birds* circling around us?

What did I *just* say about *relaxing*?

Aya, you two...

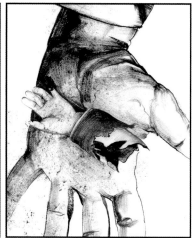

It's gone *too* far, Haloran.

We have to *tell* them.

No, Tom, we would lose them *both.* We must continue on.

123

The *Baron*, was...in my dream.

Buglings use their venom as a kind of...voice mail system for secret messages.

He made me promise we'd head to some place called Harker's Drop...

He said you'd appreciate the tactics of it.

I'd admire it *more* if the idea had come from *any* other source.

Harker's is a bottomless chasm that abuts the Vespertine's seat of power...

...but... the many narrow rope bridges should very much level the odds against any attack.

It has to be a *trap*. The Baron serves the *enemy*, remember.

The Baron serves *himself* above all others. He could have turned us in at *any* time.

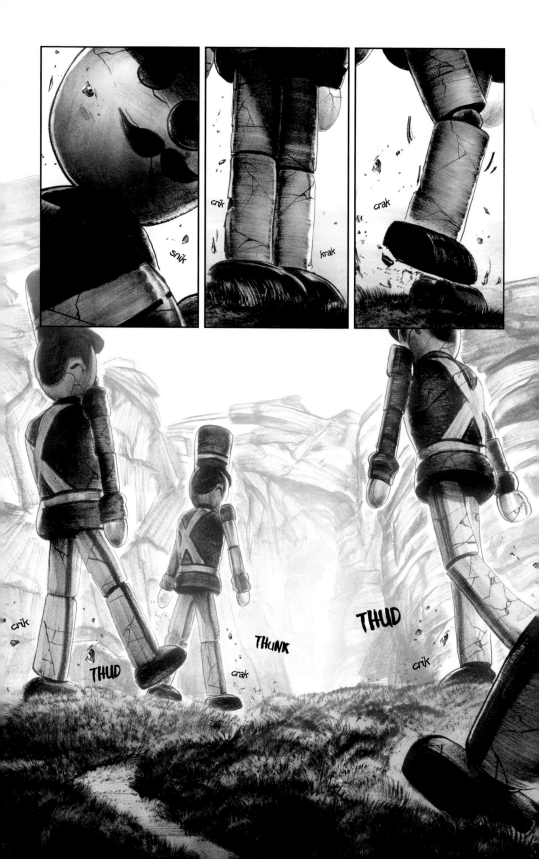

143

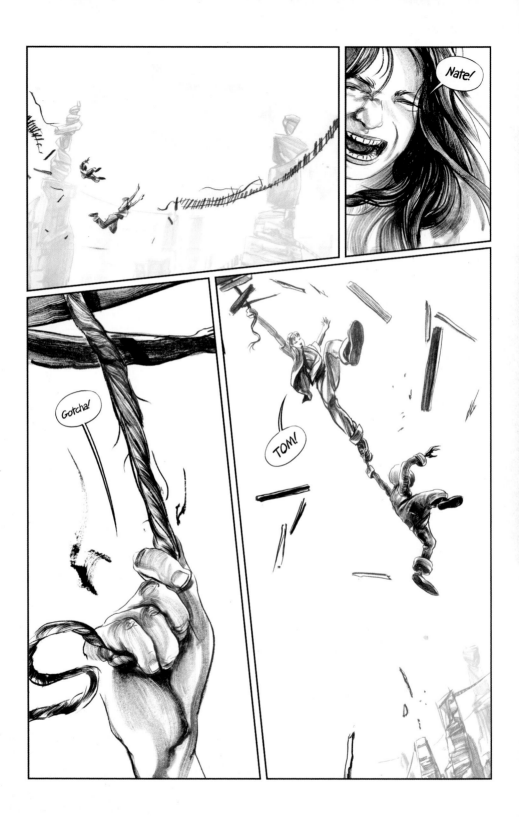

The Vespertine commands you to *remain* here and observe.

Commands!

Now *that* does sound serious.

Seems like the *Ten Men* feel the *same.*

I presume this means I am under *arrest* again?

I'm afraid so, sir.

And that's why you're on the wrong side of this.

Watch your *mount*... I hear the birds are a bit *sweet* on the girl-ape.

What do you think will *follow* when our dear leader achieves his *revenge,* Private?

I'm sure I don't know, sir.

'swear it.

I...don't believe you.

Ow!

Clever Girl.

No!

I am *not* your *father*, Walt.

Walt?

I am something *much* more terrible...

I am the *Vespertine's.*

Haloran, *NO!!*

Ahh!

What's all this?

You let him go, Nate. After *everything* Walt did. After all that he was *going* to do.

I... *had* to, Tabitha. You *saw* him.

He's not a...*threat* anymore.

...You'd better be *right*...

...for *all* our sakes.

Now get some *rest.* First day of *school* tomorrow.

Jeez... that's *right.*

Try *not* to be *late.* Old Mrs. Choat is a total *beast* if you're *tardy.*

Removing the Vespertine has unleashed a *torrent*, Tom. This is a *new* game now.

Only *you* would be so petty as to see this as a mere *game*, Baron.

A game is *exactly* what this is...

...and I *do* intend to *survive* it, my dear Tom... as I *always* do.

Savor this moment of respite. It won't last long.

The machine of *war* has begun its turning...

...You have *two* guardians to train now...

...and only *one* chance to get it *right* before the Shadows *return*.

The End